FLY TO THE RESCUE!

the TiNY GENiUSES

FLY TO THE RESCUE!

by Megan E. Bryant

Scholastic Inc.

ISBN 978-0-545-90951-8

10 9 8 7 6 5 4 3   18 19 20 21 22

Printed in the U.S.A.   40
First printing 2018

Book design by Maeve Norton

FOR CLARA,
WHO MAKES MY HEART SOAR

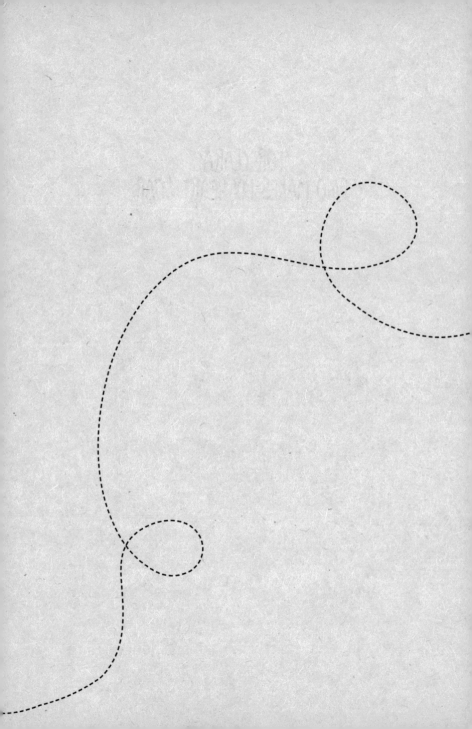

CHAPTER 1

Jake Everdale stared at the clock above Ms. Turner's head. That clock was the coolest thing in his fourth-grade classroom. It didn't just show the hours and minutes. It even counted the seconds and milliseconds, which meant something on it was always moving—just like Jake.

That's not why Jake was watching the clock, though. With one glance, those bright-red numbers told him exactly how much longer until school got out. And right now, at this very moment, the clock said 2:59:07:11. Just 53.49 seconds to go and school would be over. For the first time all day, Jake let himself feel hopeful. *Maybe Ms. Turner will forget to give back our quizzes*, he thought. *Maybe she didn't have time to grade them.*

2:59:19:52.

"You should all be making progress on your science projects," Ms. Turner was saying—but Jake wasn't listening.

2:59:33:16.

"If you have questions, now is the time to ask them," she continued. "Don't wait until the last minute."

2:59:41:52.

Almost there! Jake cheered to himself.

"And one more thing . . ." Ms. Turner said. "I have your quizzes from yesterday."

NO! Jake wanted to yell. The truth was, Jake didn't need to get his quiz back to know that he'd failed. And sure enough, there was a bright-red F at the top of the paper—and a line under it for his parents to sign. Jake crumpled up the quiz and stuffed it into his backpack as fast as he could. But he wasn't fast enough, because he heard a familiar laugh from the next desk.

"Nice work, Everdale . . . or maybe we should call you Ever*fail*," sneered Aiden Allen. Everyone sitting around them started to giggle. Aiden Allen got As in everything. Even his initials were A.A. But in the personality department, Aiden was a solid F.

At 3:00:00:00, Jake was the first one out the door. As Jake walked home from school, his backpack felt heavier with every step he took. With one quiz, his day had gone from good to bad. Another lecture from Mom and Dad . . . another night of no TV after dinner . . . another punishment.

The worst part was that Jake had really tried this time. He studied at his desk for a whole hour. He read his science notes four different times. He even made flash cards. But during the quiz, everything he knew flew out of his brain like the baseball he homered over the fence last week.

Jake decided there was only one thing left to try: the Wishing Well behind Franklin Elementary School.

Technically, it wasn't a wishing well at all—just a muddy old storm drain. But everybody at school knew it was more than that. If the stories were true, the Wishing Well could grant any wish. But you had to give up something in return—and not just anything. No, it had to be your favorite, most special possession. If you closed your eyes, spun around three times, and threw it into the well— *poof!* Your wish would come true. The catch, though, was that you only got one chance. Jake had been waiting to make a wish since kindergarten. He didn't want to waste it.

But now, Jake had a feeling that it was time.

"Hey, Mom," Jake yelled as he ran inside, dropping his backpack on the floor. His dog, Flapjack, was waiting at the door, wagging his tail wildly. Jake paused to give Flapjack a quick pet, then thundered upstairs without bothering to take off his raincoat or his muddy sneakers.

"Hi, honey," Mom called. "Did you get your quiz back?"

Jake pretended he hadn't heard her as he searched his room. *My best, most special thing*, he thought. Well, that was easy—it was his collection of signed baseball cards, of course. But there was no way Jake could bear to throw them into the Wishing Well.

Suddenly, Jake spotted a pile of plastic figures Aunt Margaret had sent for his birthday. The Heroes of History set included a bunch of famous people, from scientists to explorers to artists, from across the centuries. Jake might have been more interested if the Heroes came with cool accessories, like remote-controlled vehicles or tiny chemistry sets. But they didn't. They just stood there.

I guess they're special, Jake thought, staring at the plastic figures. *After all, Aunt Margaret gave them to me.* As the world's top neuroscientist, Aunt Margaret knew more about the human brain than anybody else. When she wasn't at work in her lab, she was traveling all over the globe to give speeches or receive awards for her amazing discoveries. Jake and his family almost never saw her . . . which meant she would never know that he'd gotten rid of her present.

Jake stuffed the Heroes of History into his pockets. Then he raced down the stairs and was about to crash through the back door when—

"Jake! Your quiz?" Mom called from the kitchen.

"In-my-backpack-gotta-go!" Jake yelled in a rush as he flew out the door.

Jake ran down the sidewalk—past the house where his best friend, Emerson Lewis, lived; past the playground; and just past Franklin Elementary School to the grassy field behind it. Usually,

Franklin Field was packed with kids playing, but today, it was closed. Five days of nonstop rain had turned it into a mud pit.

The storm drain—the Wishing Well—was at the far edge of the field, right where the sidewalk stopped. Jake peered through the sturdy metal grate, but it was so dark down there that he couldn't see anything. He could hear the sound of water flowing through it, though.

Jake clapped his hands over his eyes, spun around three times, and took a deep breath.

"Uh, Wishing Well?" Jake began. "I, uh . . ."

Somewhere in the distance, Jake heard a low rumble of thunder. A prickly feeling ran down his neck, making him shiver even though the autumn day was warm.

"I—uh—" he tried again.

More thunder. Louder, this time.

Closer.

"I-wish-for-better-grades-in-school!" Jake said.

Then, with his eyes tightly shut, he threw the Heroes of History into the storm drain. Every last one.

Crack! The thunder was so loud it rattled in Jake's bones.

Jake's eyes flew open. All of a sudden, a flash of lightning tore through the dark clouds and hit the padlock on the gate of Franklin Field, sending sparks flying—and Jake running. But Jake wasn't fast enough to beat the rain. He was completely drenched before he was even halfway home. And that was what made Jake realize something: He had thrown the Heroes of History into the swirling waters of the storm drain—but he had never heard a splash.

The storm, Jake told himself. *There was too much thunder to hear anything else.*

But inside, he wasn't so sure.

CHAPTER 2

When Jake got home, Mom was waiting at the door with a towel in her hand. She did not look happy.

"Go dry off," she said. "Then we're going to have a talk."

Jake's sneakers went *squish-squish-squish* as he trudged inside. Upstairs, he took a long time to change his clothes. But he had to face Mom eventually. Jake found her in the kitchen, cooking dinner while his little sister, Julia, got a head start on her homework.

When Jake sat next to his sister at the kitchen table, he spotted his failed quiz—which made him feel even worse.

"Well, Jake?" Mom began. "What do you have to say for yourself?"

Jake stared at the table.

"You're not giving me any choice but to take away video games," Mom said. "And . . . baseball."

"What?" Jake yelped. "Mom! No!"

"You know it's against the rules to go somewhere without permission," Mom said. "I was worried about you! And now this quiz? Another F?"

"But that's why I left!" Jake interrupted her. "I—I went back to school. To ask for extra help."

It wasn't completely untrue.

Mom looked surprised. "You did?"

Jake nodded. "I know I have to do better," he told her. "I studied really hard. But it wasn't enough. I'm too dumb."

All of a sudden, Mom didn't seem mad anymore. "Oh, Jake," she said with a sigh. "You're not dumb."

"Please don't make me quit baseball," Jake said. "It's my favorite thing in the world."

"I know," Mom said gently. "But we've talked about how things change in fourth grade. The work can be more challenging. Baseball is a big commitment. All those practices and games take up a lot of time when you could be studying."

"But—there's still my science fair project!" Jake exclaimed. "The science project counts for more than the quizzes! If I get a really good grade, can I stay on the team?"

Mom didn't say anything.

"Please?" Jake begged.

"Okay," Mom finally said. "But if you don't do well, you'll have to take a break from baseball."

Jake stood up so fast his chair scraped across the floor. "I promise I'll do better," he said. "I'll get started right now!"

"I can't wait to see what you come up with!"

Mom said, smiling for the first time since Jake got home.

Jake took the stairs two at a time and bounded into his room. He got a fresh piece of paper and sharpened his favorite pencil, the one with the baseball-shaped eraser. But where were the science fair instructions? Jake searched the whole room before he found them crumpled up under the bed. Then Jake broke into the supersecret candy stash in his underwear drawer. Nobody knew about it—not even Emerson. At last, Jake had everything he needed: paper, pencil, instructions, chocolate. Jake knew he was going to have the best science project of all time . . . just as soon as he came up with a brilliant idea.

Then he heard a knock at the door. Mom was standing in the hallway with the phone in her hand. "Emerson has a homework question," she whispered, handing it to him. "You have two minutes to talk."

"Hello?" Jake said into the phone.

"What did your mom say about the quiz?" Emerson asked.

"She's pretty mad," Jake replied. "If I don't get a good grade on my science project, she'll make me quit the team."

"No way!" Emerson howled.

"I know," Jake replied miserably.

"You'd better get to work," Emerson said. "What's your project about?"

"I'm just about to figure that out," Jake said. "Do you have any ideas?"

"My project's about the weather," Emerson said. "And Hannah's doing a really cool one about how plants grow."

"Plants! I could do that!" Jake said excitedly.

"Yeah, but Hannah started, like, a month ago," Emerson pointed out.

Jake's smiled faded. "Right. I forgot that seeds take a while to grow."

Mom appeared in the doorway again and tapped her watch.

"I gotta go," Jake told Emerson. "See you tomorrow."

After Mom left, Jake smoothed out the instructions and started to read. *Background Research . . . Bibliography . . . Hypothesis . . . Procedure . . .*

Jake frowned. He wasn't sure what half those words meant. All he knew for certain was that he was way behind. Jake didn't have a clue where to begin. The school year had just started and he already felt like he was hopelessly behind.

A prickly, panicky feeling started in Jake's stomach. Then it spread through his entire body. There was nothing Jake could do to stop it. Worst of all was knowing that he was probably going to fail. Again. That meant he would let down the whole baseball team . . . and Coach Carlson . . . and even his parents.

And it was all his own fault.

I really am a dummy, Jake thought angrily. *Not even the Wishing Well can help a dummy like me.*

Jake threw his pencil onto the desk. "I wish someone could just do this for me!" he cried.

POP!

A bright flash of light in the middle of Jake's desk exploded into hundreds of small, burning sparks. They were just like the ones from the lightning bolt that had hit the padlock back at Franklin Field. *Oh no!* he thought desperately. His desk was a wreck, cluttered with papers and notebooks that could catch fire—

But oddly enough, the sparks just sat there, twinkling. Nothing burst into flames—not even the science fair instructions.

Jake waved his hands through the air to get rid of the smoke. When it finally cleared, he saw something so amazing—so astonishing—

There was a tiny person—a man—standing in the middle of Jake's desk. He wore fancy, old-fashioned clothes, with a ruffled shirt and a silk vest. His long hair tumbled around his shoulders as he peered up at Jake.

"Excuse me, young sir," he finally said, speaking in a clipped English accent. "Would you be so kind as to direct me to the lecture hall?"

The lecture hall? Jake thought in confusion.

"Pip, pip," the man said, clapping his hands impatiently. "I haven't got all day!"

Jake finally found his voice. "Who—who *are* you?" he asked.

The man pulled himself up to his whole height—about three inches tall. "Me?" he asked incredulously, as though he couldn't believe Jake didn't recognize him. "*Me?* Why, I am Sir Isaac Newton."

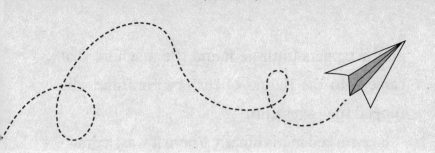

CHAPTER 3

Jake closed his eyes. *When I open my eyes, everything will be normal again*, he told himself.

Slowly, Jake opened his eyes—but nothing had changed. Sir Isaac was still scowling up at him, tapping his foot. But he didn't just look annoyed . . . he also looked familiar.

"Hold on," Jake said as he dove into the clutter under his desk. Jake dug through his rock collection and his spare cleats and about a hundred gum wrappers until he found the brochure that came with the Heroes of History. He frantically flipped the pages until—

Jake sucked in his breath. There it was: a drawing labeled "Sir Isaac Newton," a perfect match to the tiny person standing on Jake's desk. The man in the drawing had the same bottle-green vest, the same wavy hair, and the same brass-buckled shoes.

"This can't be happening," Jake whispered. His eyes darted back and forth as he began to read.

> *Sir Isaac Newton*
> *1642–1727, England*
> *Sir Isaac Newton was one of the greatest scientists of all time. Truly a Hero of History!*

The Wishing Well! Jake thought gleefully. *It worked! My wish came true!*

Just not in the way Jake had expected.

This is going to be amazing, he thought. *I wished for help on my science project—and now one of the best scientists ever is here to help me!*

Just then, Jake heard a *rrrrrip* and a *clink* and a *thunk*. He glanced at his desk to find Sir Isaac sprawled across the desk in a heap of paper clips. One of the paper clips was stuck to his shoe with a piece of tape.

Jake jumped up. "What are you doing?" he asked.

With as much dignity as he could muster, Sir Isaac pulled himself to his feet. He gestured to the tape dispenser and said, in a haughty voice, "I am attempting to uncover the properties of this odd contraption."

"You . . . taped a paper clip to your shoe?" Jake asked.

Sir Isaac pretended he hadn't heard Jake as he shook his foot in a hopeless attempt to remove the paper clip. "Perhaps this will be of use," he said as he hopped over to the stapler.

"No!" Jake yelped. "Here, let me help—"

Sir Isaac didn't look happy about it, but he did let Jake pull the paper clip off his shoe.

"Thank you," he said stiffly. "Now, I really must be on my way. I'm expected in the lecture hall, and I despise lateness in any form."

"Yeah . . . about your, um, lecture," Jake began, wracking his brain. "It was, um, canceled."

"Canceled!" Sir Isaac exclaimed. His face darkened. "I suppose one of my enemies is behind this—of all the scheming, underhanded tricks—"

"No," Jake said quickly. "It was, um, by order of the, uh, queen. She needs you here instead. To solve . . . a . . . um . . . very important science problem."

Jake held his breath. Would Sir Isaac buy it?

"I see," the genius replied, sounding surprised. "Well, it's highly unusual . . . but in the name of science, I shall do my utmost to uncover the truth."

Yes! Jake cheered to himself. With a genius like Sir Isaac Newton on his side, Jake knew he'd ace his science project.

"Jake!" Mom yelled from downstairs. "Time for dinner!"

"Be right there!" he yelled back.

"And what shall I be investigating?" Sir Isaac asked.

Jake's face went blank.

Sir Isaac nodded knowingly. "It's all right, my boy, I already know why I'm here."

"You do?" Jake asked.

"To figure out why you've grown so large, of course," Sir Isaac replied.

"Jake!" Mom called again.

"I have to go, but I'll be back," Jake said. "For now, just, uh, make yourself at home. We'll get to work later."

"Later?" scoffed Sir Isaac. "No, I shall begin recording my observations right now."

As Jake left the room, he could hear Sir Isaac muttering to himself. "The subject looks to be a boy of some nine, perhaps ten years of age, quite ordinary in all respects except for his size and his slovenly chambers."

Jake smiled as he closed the door. He didn't care what Sir Isaac said . . . as long as he helped with the science project.

After dinner, Jake spent the evening sorting his baseball cards while Sir Isaac scribbled equations with the stub of a pencil. *Sir Isaac is supersmart*, Jake reminded himself whenever he felt a twinge of guilt for goofing off. *We'll still have plenty of time for the science project, even if we don't start until tomorrow.*

When it was time for bed, Jake made sure to say good night to his parents downstairs so they wouldn't find out about the miniature genius in his room. Then he climbed into bed and turned out the light. "Good night, Sir Isaac," he said in a sleepy voice.

Click!

It felt like Jake had only been asleep for a few minutes when a bright light shone in his face. He rolled over and buried his face in the pillow. "Five more minutes, Mom," he mumbled.

Click!

Suddenly, it was dark.

Click!

Then light again.

"Remarkable!" Sir Isaac breathed.

Jake sat up and rubbed his eyes. "What are you doing?" he asked.

The light kept flashing—*click, click, click*. That's when Jake realized that Sir Isaac had discovered the light switch.

"The power of the sun, under my command!" Sir Isaac marveled. "How can you sleep at a time like this?" His face shone with glee.

"It is little wonder that the queen has sent me to this land of mystery," he continued. "A land where giant children roam, a land where light has been captured and contained. Get up, so that we may begin our investigations!"

Jake flopped back down on the bed. "It's okay, Sir Isaac," he mumbled. "It's just a light. It will be here in the morning. We can investigate it tomorrow."

"One must never hesitate when given the opportunity to uncover the marvels of the universe!" Sir Isaac scolded. "If you must be a lie-abed, so be it, but I shall not rest until I learn the secret to this sorcery!"

Click!

Click!

Click!

Jake sighed and pulled the blanket over his head. It was going to be a *long* night.

CHAPTER 4

When Jake awoke the next morning, he couldn't tell if the sun was shining in his face—or if Sir Isaac had turned all the lights on. The answer, it turned out, was both. Even after Jake got ready for school, Sir Isaac was squinting his eyes as he stared directly at the blazing bulb.

"Still obsessed with the light switch, huh?" Jake asked as he searched for his reading log.

"Look here," Sir Isaac announced. "From what I

can determine, the source of this light is a globular orb of glass with some sort of silver tentacle twirled within it. If only I could examine it up close!"

"Listen," Jake began. "I have to go to school, but I have something here that's just as interesting as that lightbulb. More interesting, even!"

With a flourish, Jake presented Sir Isaac with his science fair instructions. Sir Isaac barely glanced at them before turning all his attention back to the lightbulb.

Jake felt that familiar panic mounting in his chest. *What's the point of having an actual genius here if he won't help me?* he wondered.

Suddenly, inspiration struck. Jake ran to the hall closet and grabbed a brand-new lightbulb, still in the package. Then he dashed back into his room.

"Here," he said, offering the lightbulb to Sir Isaac. "You can have this lightbulb."

That got Sir Isaac's attention. When he reached for the bulb, Jake held it just out of his reach.

"But promise me you'll look at the science fair instructions—I mean, the queen's assignment," Jake said. "I really need your help."

"Yes, yes, of course," Sir Isaac replied impatiently.

"Great," Jake said as he placed the lightbulb on the desk. "Now, I have to go to school—"

"Grammar school?" Sir Isaac said with a loud sniff. "I do pity you. Never could abide the place, myself."

"Really?" Jake asked. Could it be true that one of the world's greatest thinkers disliked school as much as Jake did?

"Of course!" Sir Isaac said. "I never could determine who was the greater half-wit, my teacher or my fellow students."

"I see," Jake said. Of course Sir Isaac didn't like school when he was young. He was too smart for his classes. *That sounds like a pretty good problem to have*, Jake thought wistfully.

"I'll be back around four o'clock. Until I get home, you should stay in my room, okay? And whatever you do, keep the door closed," Jake warned Sir Isaac. So much could go wrong. If Mom worked from her home office—if Flapjack mistook Sir Isaac for a new chew toy—

But Jake pushed all those worries out of his head as he slid down the banister. After all, Sir Isaac was one of the smartest people of all time. Surely he had enough common sense to look out for himself.

What could possibly go wrong?

When Jake got home after baseball practice, he was so excited to see what Sir Isaac had accomplished that he bounded up the stairs two at a time.

But right before he burst into his room, Jake

paused. He tapped quietly on the door, then pushed it open.

"Sir Isaac?" he called in a low voice. "I'm ba—*ahhhhh!* What have you done to my room?"

Jake was so stunned that he dropped his backpack. His room had been completely transformed—and not for the better. For starters, Sir Isaac had gotten into the paper clips again. He had strung them together in long, glinting chains that swooped down from the ceiling. Jake realized that Sir Isaac must have gone on some sort of school supplies scavenger hunt throughout the entire house.

The paper-clip garlands weren't the only clue that Sir Isaac had ignored Jake's advice and left the room. A glittering crystal bead hung from each paper clip, filling Jake's room with thousands of shimmering rainbows. Jake recognized the beads almost immediately: They came from Julia's favorite sparkly tiara.

Jake gulped. *This is bad*, he thought.

"Greetings, young squire!" Sir Isaac exclaimed from Jake's desk.

"We have to take all this stuff down and put Julia's tiara back together again," Jake said.

"Take it down?" Sir Isaac replied. "In case you failed to notice, I am in the midst of an experiment!"

"For the queen's assignment?" Jake asked him doubtfully. Was this crazy rainbow-crystal-paper-clip contraption supposed to be the science project Jake would present to the whole school?

Sir Isaac looked confused. "No, I haven't had time for that," he said. "Not when I'm in the midst of splitting beams of light into the spectrum of visible color—"

"Jake!"

Julia's voice was halfway between a shout and a shriek. Too late, Jake realized that he'd accidentally left the bedroom door wide open.

And Julia, in the doorway, had just discovered what had happened to her favorite tiara.

"What did you do?" she screeched.

"Shhh!" Jake panicked. "Don't tell—"

"MOM!" she screamed.

"Work it out, you two." Mom's voice floated up the stairs.

Jake grabbed Julia's hand and yanked her into his room, then shut the door behind them.

"What did you do to my tiara?" Julia said as her cheeks turned bright red. "You wrecked it!"

"Please, Julia," begged Jake. "You can't tell Mom or Dad or—or—or anyone! I swear, it wasn't me!"

Julia's eyes narrowed. She opened her mouth to yell for Mom again.

Jake had no choice but to tell her everything. "It was him," he said, pointing at the tiny genius on his desk.

"Him?" Julia asked. "One of your dolls from Aunt Margaret?"

"A doll?" sniffed Sir Isaac. "Young lady, I am Sir Isaac Newton, Fellow of Trinity College at Cambridge University and Lucasian Professor of Mathematics at Cambridge, president of the Royal Society of London, and member of Parliament."

Julia looked suspicious. "It talks?" she asked. "I didn't know it had batteries."

"No batteries," Jake said. "He's—well—he's alive."

The expression on Julia's face shifted like a kaleidoscope, going from anger to shock to disbelief to, at last, wonder. "I want it!" she said. "Trade?"

"No way," Jake replied, shaking his head.

Julia's lower lip stuck out in a pout. "But it was my favorite-best tiara," she said in a small voice.

"Don't cry," Jake said. "I'll—I'll save my allowance and buy you a new tiara. How about that?"

Julia shook her head as a single tear slipped down her face. "I want him," she said firmly.

"No," Jake said, louder than he meant. "He stays in my room."

Julia's lip quivered.

"But you can play with him whenever you want," Jake quickly added. "Okay?"

Julia grinned. Then, suddenly, she ducked into the hall. A few moments later, Jake heard a loud *thunk—thunk—thunk*. He peeked out of his room to see Julia dragging her dollhouse toward his bedroom.

"What are you doing?" Jake asked.

"Mr. Newton can live in my dollhouse," Julia said. "It's just his size."

"Absolutely not," Jake began. But before he could finish his sentence, Sir Isaac's face lit up.

"Splendid!" he exclaimed as he examined the bright-pink dollhouse, which had three stories, working lights, and a doorbell that played "The Itsy-Bitsy Spider." "These accommodations are grander than I ever anticipated, and I thank you, kind miss."

"You're welcome!" Julia replied as she hoisted the dollhouse onto Jake's desk—dropping it right on the science fair instructions. "Would you like some tea?"

"Why, yes, I believe a cup of tea would be just the thing," Newton replied.

Jake stifled the urge to groan as he buried his head in his hands. From the twinkling crystals to the shimmering rainbows to the doll-sized mansion, he barely even recognized his room anymore!

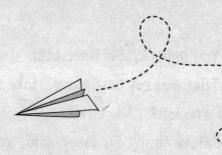

CHAPTER 5

The next day, things got even worse. When Jake got home from school, he discovered his favorite baseball glove in tatters.

"Sir Isaac!" Jake howled. "What have you done?"

Sir Isaac popped his head out from under the lampshade. He was wearing a protective leather smock that looked awfully familiar. It was made out of Jake's glove!

"You're back," Sir Isaac said.

"That was my best glove," Jake said. "Why did you wreck it?"

"Safety first," Sir Isaac said, gesturing to his smock. "The temperature cast from the bulb is exceedingly hot. Now I will be protected from the heat."

"That's wonderful," Jake said sarcastically. "I'm glad you have so much time to spend with a lightbulb."

"As am I!" Sir Isaac agreed. "Now, boy, I have an important task for you."

"For the queen's assignment?" Jake asked hopefully.

"Oh, no," Sir Isaac said with a wave of his hand. From the pocket of his protective smock, he pulled a miniature scroll of paper. "I am in need of some additional materials for the next stage of my investigations."

Jake pinched the tiny list between his thumb

and forefinger and squinted as he tried to read it. "Calipers? Scales? Sealing wax?" he read. "I don't know what half of these things do."

"You don't have to know what they do," Sir Isaac said. "You just have to fetch them."

"I'm not getting you anything else until you at least *look* at these instructions!" Jake said. He walked out of his room, slamming the door behind him. The science fair was in a couple of days, and Jake was even further behind than when he'd first wished for help. Jake wandered into the kitchen, where Dad was starting to cook dinner.

"Hey, champ," Dad said. "What's up?"

"Just getting a snack," Jake replied glumly as he took an apple out of the fruit bowl.

"How's that science project going?" Dad asked.

Jake forced himself to smile. "Good," he said—a little too quickly. "It's, uh, pretty interesting stuff."

"Fantastic!" Dad said. "I'd love to take a look. After dinner, do you want to show me what you've done so far?"

"No!" Jake yelped. "I want it to be a surprise."

"I see," Dad said, nodding. "Sounds very exciting! Maybe I'll see if Aunt Margaret can come."

"She's probably too busy," Jake said right away. "It's just the fourth-grade science fair."

"Your aunt always loved the science fair when she was growing up," Dad said. "I'll email her later to see if she has time. I bet she'd get a kick out of coming back to the Franklin Elementary School science fair."

"Great," Jake said weakly. *Sir Isaac* has *to help me*, Jake thought. He took a big bite of his apple as he trudged back upstairs. But at the top of the stairs, Jake paused. He sniffed the air. What was that strange smell?

Oh no, Jake thought in a panic as he raced to his room. Flapjack was scratching at the door, whining anxiously. Now Jake was sure that something was seriously wrong—and it was all his fault for leaving Sir Isaac alone!

Jake burst into his room and looked around. Everything seemed fine. Julia was calmly hanging toilet-paper curtains in the dollhouse.

"Julia," Jake said urgently, "what is that smell?"

"I think it's Sir Isaac's experiment," she replied without looking up.

Jake glanced over at the lamp next to his bed, where Sir Isaac was holding a bright-red crayon right next to the lightbulb. The crayon sizzled as it started to melt from the white-hot bulb, leaving a shiny red patch of molten wax on Jake's desk.

"My dear girl, would you bring me the blue one?" Sir Isaac asked Julia.

Jake crossed the room and yanked the crayon out of Sir Isaac's hands. "Do you guys have any idea how dangerous this is?" he yelled.

"The only thing to fear is ignorance." Sir Isaac sniffed. "If the greatest discoveries must be born of the greatest danger, so be it."

"Easy for you to say," Jake muttered. "You're not about to be grounded for all eternity. Won't you *please* look at these instructions with me? I really need some help—" Jake waved the instructions, which he'd retrieved earlier from under the dollhouse.

"My mind will not be quieted until I have discovered all the secrets of the spectrum," Sir Isaac declared.

Jake took a deep breath—and a huge bite of his apple. *Crunch!* Flecks of apple sprayed across his desk. A look of disgust crossed Sir Isaac's face as he brushed a piece of apple off his leather smock. But when Sir Isaac realized what Jake was eating, his expression shifted to panic.

"Good heavens, boy, what's wrong with you?" Sir Isaac exclaimed, scrambling backward across Jake's desk. "Take care with that thing!"

"It's just an apple," Jake said.

"It's an apple the size of a haystack!" Sir Isaac shouted back. "An apple that size could *kill* a man if it fell on him!"

Those words sparked something in Jake's memory. "That's how you discovered gravity, isn't it?" he asked. "You were in an orchard or something, and an apple fell on your head and you wondered—*why?*"

Sir Isaac's shoulders stiffened. "You've got it half right," he said. "But the apple didn't fall on my head. I saw one fall from the tree outside my bedroom window and wanted to know why apples—or anything else, for that matter—fall in just one direction. Nothing falls sideways, you know, or upwards. They always fall *down.*"

"That's amazing," Jake said. "I mean, that's one of the greatest discoveries ever . . . and it came from something so ordinary."

"The world is full of wondrous miracles—for

those who want to see them," Sir Isaac replied. "Now, I'd thank you to dispose of that apple."

"Throw away my apple?" Jake asked. "No. I'm going to finish eating it. This is *my* room, after all."

In an angry huff, Sir Isaac pulled off his smock and threw it down. "You can solve your own scientific inquiries, then!" he snapped.

"No!" Jake exclaimed. "Wait—"

But Sir Isaac had already stalked off to the dollhouse and pulled the toilet-paper curtains closed with a *whoosh*.

"Arrrgghhh!" Jake groaned. A genius-level tantrum was the *last* thing he needed.

"You weren't very nice," Julia told him.

"He's the one who's not very nice!" Jake protested. "All he's done since he got here is insult me and order me around! Why are you taking his side anyway?"

"He told me I could be his helper!" Julia said.

"But he was supposed to be *my* helper!" Jake

exclaimed. Then he shook his head. "Forget it. Obviously, I'm on my own. If only . . ."

"What?" asked Julia.

"Nothing." Jake sighed. "I just wish I had a different helper."

POP!

CHAPTER 6

Jake dashed across the room, waving his arms wildly through the thick cloud of smoke. As the air began to clear, he saw movement among the sparks that were still glittering on his desk. A small woman, no bigger than three inches tall, pulled herself to her feet and dusted off her leather coat.

"Now *that* was a bumpy landing," she said, peering through a pair of goggles that was strapped to her face. "Must've been ejected on impact. Where's the *Canary*?"

Julia squealed with delight. "You brought your *pet*?" she cried.

The woman chuckled. "I suppose you could say that," she replied. "The *Canary* is my airplane. Bright yellow, she practically named herself. Any sign of her?"

I don't think you traveled here by plane, Jake thought. But what he said was: "Wait a second. Who *are* you, exactly?"

The woman crossed his desk with long strides and held out her hand. "I'm Amelia Earhart," she declared.

"The famous pilot," Jake realized as his mouth dropped open. He carefully took hold of her tiny hand to shake it. "I'm Jake Everdale. This is my sister, Julia."

"A pleasure to meet you both," Miss Earhart said. She swept her long white scarf over her shoulder.

Jake wracked his brain, trying to remember everything he'd heard about Amelia Earhart before. Her daring sense of adventure had led her to become one of the first woman pilots. She'd set lots of new records and broken several others. But something had gone terribly wrong on her final flight. Miss Earhart—and her plane—had vanished without a trace.

Sir Isaac poked his head out from the toilet-paper curtains. "Pilot of what?" he asked rudely. "No one in their right mind would let a *woman* set foot on a ship."

Miss Earhart pulled off her goggles and narrowed her eyes. "It's small-minded thinking like that that got us into this fix, where men want to do everything themselves and never give a girl a chance," she said, waggling her finger. "You ought to know that a woman can do anything a man can do—even fly an airplane."

"Fly?" Sir Isaac asked. "Like a bird? Preposterous!"

"It is not!" Miss Earhart countered, pulling herself up to her full height. "I'll have you know that I was the very first woman to fly solo across the Atlantic and the first *person* to fly solo across the Pacific Ocean."

"A mortal—man *or* woman—flying through the air," Sir Isaac said, laughing like he'd heard a great joke. "The very idea! Dear lady, I realize that you may be given to flights of fancy, but there is a force, you see, that draws objects *down* to the surface of the earth. I have decided to call it 'gravity,' after the Latin word *gravitas*, meaning 'weight'—"

"I know all about gravity," Miss Earhart said.

Now Sir Isaac looked even more astonished. "*You* know about gravity?" he asked. "That's even more absurd than the thought that you have flown through the air in some sort of nature-defying contraption!"

Miss Earhart turned to Julia. "Can you believe him?" she asked. "Don't listen to a word he says.

There's plenty of unenlightened men out there who'd rather stand in our way than get out of it. But we won't allow them to hold us back, will we?"

"Unenlightened?" Sir Isaac sputtered as his face turned bright red. "You cause me offense! I have dedicated my *life* to the pursuit of knowledge!"

As the two tiny geniuses launched into a full-fledged argument, Jake buried his head in his hands. "This is a disaster!" He groaned.

"Maybe they would get along better if they had a big project to work on together," Julia suggested.

"Yeah—like my science project," Jake muttered. "But Sir Isaac's not interested in helping me, and he and Miss Earhart won't stop arguing long enough for me to even *ask* her if she'd take a look!"

Jake gestured at the two geniuses, who were shouting in each other's faces.

"And if such a thing as human flight *were* possible, it would be someone like *me* who would accomplish it!" Sir Isaac hollered.

"I'd like to see you try!" Miss Earhart yelled back.

A strange, wistful look suddenly crossed Sir Isaac's face. "Yes," he said in a quiet voice. "I think I should like that as well."

Sir Isaac wishes he could fly! Jake realized all of a sudden. Miss Earhart must have realized it, too, because the scowl on her face softened.

"Why didn't you say so?" she asked. "I'm certain that can be arranged."

Sir Isaac looked skeptical, but there was a new spark of hope in his eyes. "How?" he asked, his curiosity getting the better of him.

"First we'll find the *Canary*," Miss Earhart began, ticking the steps off on her fingers. "After a landing like that, I'm sure the old girl will need some fixing, but that's nothing I haven't managed before. Then it's off we go—next stop, the wild blue yonder!"

That was all it took for Jake to have the best, brightest, most brilliant idea of his entire life. *An airplane*, he thought as a tornado of ideas whirled through his mind. *A real-life miniature airplane can be my science project!*

"Hang on a second," he said in a rush. "If you can't find the *Canary*, do you think you could *make* a new plane?"

Miss Earhart tapped her chin thoughtfully. "With the right tools, just about anything is possible. Yes, young man, if you have the supplies, we can build it."

"Yes!" Jake cheered, so loudly that Sir Isaac, Miss Earhart, and even Julia jumped.

At last, Jake had solved the problem that had been worrying him for days!

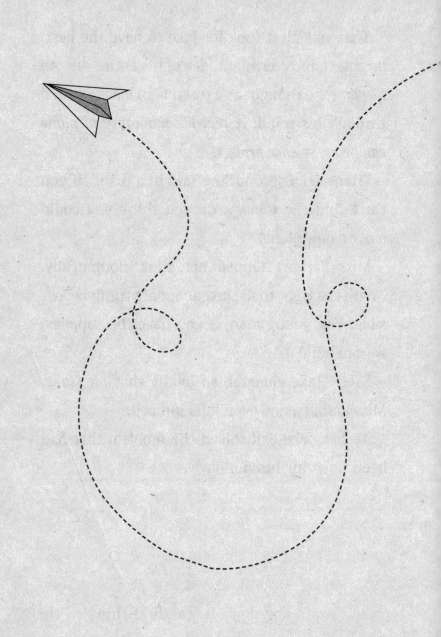

CHAPTER 7

"Jake!"

Jake bolted upright at once. "What?" he asked sleepily. He tried to jump out of bed, but the blankets were all tangled around his legs. He landed on the floor with a loud *thunk*.

"Get down here *right now*!"

"Coming!" Jake yelled back.

What did I do? Jake wondered as he stumbled toward the door. It was first thing in the morning. He hadn't even had time to get into trouble yet!

When Jake reached the living room, though, it only took one look to know exactly why Dad was so mad. The floor was covered with a massive mess of broken glass, tangled wires, and itty-bitty LED lights.

"Whoa," Jake whispered. "What happened?"

"That's what we want to know, young man," Mom said, standing in the doorway with her hands on her hips. "What happened to the TV?"

Jake's heart pulsed with pure panic. He could make a pretty good guess about who, exactly, was responsible for this disaster—and why they had done it. But how could he tell Mom and Dad about Sir Isaac and Miss Earhart?

Jake swallowed hard. There was only one thing to do.

"Sorry," he said, his voice barely louder than a whisper. "I didn't mean to destroy everything."

"What could have *possibly* possessed you to take apart the TV?" Mom asked. She spoke very slowly, as if she were trying to control her temper.

"I was . . . um . . . working on my science project?" Jake guessed. "I needed some supplies . . . like electronics stuff . . . and it was the middle of the night . . ."

He glanced hopefully from Mom to Dad. Would he be in less trouble if they knew it was for his science project? There was absolutely no doubt in his mind that Sir Isaac and Miss Earhart were behind this mess—especially when Jake noticed Miss Earhart's scarf, no bigger than a Band-Aid, draped across the busted remote control.

"You came downstairs in the middle of the night to dismantle the television?" Dad asked. "Jake, what were you thinking?"

"I don't know," Jake said miserably. "I just—I really want to do well on my science project.

I didn't think I could wait until today to get the stuff I needed."

Mom and Dad exchanged a troubled glance.

"We're really glad that you're so determined to succeed on your science project," Mom finally said. "But, Jake, you have to know this isn't okay."

Jake exhaled in relief.

"You'll have to be punished," Dad said. "Even though it was for your schoolwork, you know better than to destroy things."

"Are you going to take away baseball?" Jake asked urgently. "I'll pay for a new TV. I'll walk dogs and wash cars and—and anything I can do to earn some money."

"It looks like you already managed to take away TV," Dad said, a glimmer of mischief in his eyes. "So we'll have to think of something else."

Jake almost cracked a smile—almost.

"We're not sure what your punishment will be yet," Mom said. "But probably not baseball. The deal was that you could keep playing baseball as long as you did well on your science project. And it seems like you're trying very hard to uphold your end of the bargain."

"But no more of this nonsense, okay?" Dad said as he stooped down to pick up the broken glass. "We expect you to be on your best behavior—even if you are channeling your inner mad scientist these days."

"You got it," Jake promised. "No more nonsense."

Suddenly, Dad noticed Miss Earhart's scarf. A look of confusion crossed his face. "What's that?" he asked.

"Doll clothes," Jake blurted out. "It belongs to Julia. I'll take it upstairs."

"Hurry up and get ready for school," Mom called after him as Jake escaped from the living room. "We're already behind schedule."

In his room, Jake breathed a sigh of relief. That was a close call. He glanced around his room, but Sir Isaac and Miss Earhart were nowhere to be seen: not on his desk, not in Julia's dollhouse, and not even messing around with the lights. In fact, the room seemed completely empty—except for Jake himself.

"Miss Earhart? Sir Isaac?" Jake called, as loudly as he dared. "Where are you guys?"

But there was no response.

Now Jake was really starting to panic. What if Sir Isaac and Miss Earhart were lost in the house? What if Mom found them? Or worst of all—Flapjack?

"Sir Isaac!" Jake called one more time. "Miss Earhart!"

Suddenly, Jake heard a rustling noise. He dropped to his knees and peered under the bed—and could hardly believe his eyes. Somehow, overnight, Sir Isaac and Miss Earhart had set up an entire workshop—and Jake had slept through the whole thing! There were work stations made from playing cards; stools made from spools of thread; itty-bitty screws and tools that must've come from Dad's eyeglass repair kit; and a random pile of other household objects: buttons and game pieces and thumbtacks and tokens and a mountain of cotton swabs. There was even, Jake realized with a sinking feeling, a blowtorch made from a birthday candle.

"What—what—*how*—?" Jake sputtered.

At the sound of his voice, Miss Earhart looked up. "Morning!" she said in a chipper voice.

"I have to talk to you both," Jake said.

As soon as Miss Earhart and Sir Isaac were back on his desk, Jake launched into his lecture.

"What were you thinking?" he began, surprised at how much he suddenly sounded like his parents. "What you did last night was incredibly dangerous!"

"Nonsense," Sir Isaac scoffed as he examined a copper wire twined through a button. "We took all the necessary precautions."

"Before or after you pulled the TV off the wall?" Jake asked.

"Well, now, let me be the first to apologize for that," Miss Earhart spoke up. "We were just hoping to—"

"Wait," Jake interrupted her, squinting his eyes as he peeked under the bed again. "Are those burned-out birthday candles? No, never mind, don't tell me. I don't even want to know. But please promise me you won't light anything else on fire. *Please?*"

"That was her fault!" Sir Isaac crowed, pointing his finger at Miss Earhart. "I told her that you sleep quite well—quite *loudly*, I might add—with the entire room illuminated!"

"I was trying to keep the room dark enough for Jake to get some rest," Miss Earhart protested. "I used to be a nurse's aide, you know. I know what I'm talking about. Children need a good night's sleep to succeed!"

Jake, however, wasn't listening. *What am I going to do?* he wondered. Sir Isaac and Miss Earhart were completely out of control. How could Jake possibly leave them at home after all the mischief they'd gotten into?

Jake knew what he had to do. He didn't want to—but he didn't really have a choice.

"Get your coats," he told the geniuses. "You're going to school."

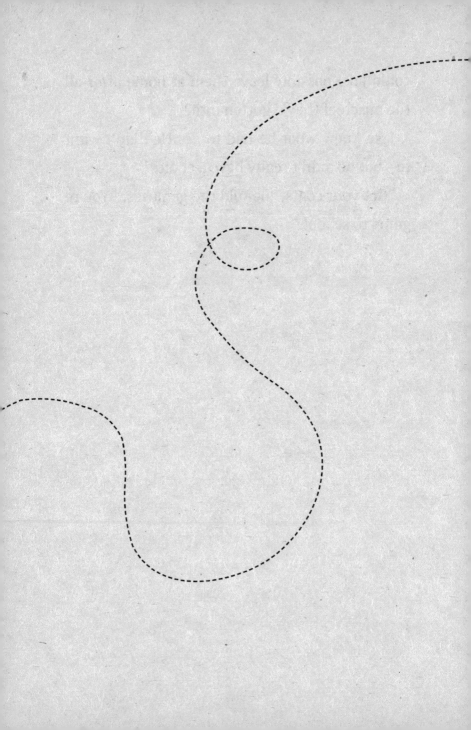

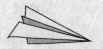

CHAPTER 8

Jake had never loved his backpack more than he did that morning. It had not one, not two, but *three* secret pockets inside. There was more than enough room for Miss Earhart and Sir Isaac to spread out, get comfortable, and relax until the school day ended. To be on the safe side, Jake decided to travel light, leaving his lunch and school books at home. Hot lunch was gross, but it was worth eating it if he didn't have to worry about his tiny geniuses being crushed by a cookie or smushed under a sandwich.

About a block away from Franklin Elementary School, Jake peeked into his backpack to check on them. He grinned when he saw each one hard at work building a miniscule component of the plane's engine. Hopefully, their tasks would keep them busy—and out of trouble—for the rest of the day.

"Now, listen," Jake said for the umpteenth time, "you guys have *got* to stay in my backpack until we get home. All day. No exceptions. If anybody sees you—"

"I assure you, boy, I have no interest in wasting my day at your school," Sir Isaac interrupted, not even bothering to look up from the electrode in his hands. "My own school days were tedious enough."

"We're here to help you, Jake, not make more problems!" Miss Earhart said brightly. Jake tried to return her smile. *We just have to get through the science fair on Friday*, Jake reminded himself. *One more day.*

"Okay," Jake said in a low voice. "Let's go."

When Jake arrived in Ms. Turner's classroom, the clock read 8:29:54:12. He was less than six seconds away from getting a tardy! Jake slid into his seat right before the bell rang.

"Safe!" Ms. Turner joked, spreading her arms like an umpire. The whole class laughed, and even Jake smiled as he carefully tucked his backpack under the desk.

"Books closed. Papers out. Pencils up," Ms. Turner announced.

Jake's smile disappeared. Those were the worst six words to hear first thing in the morning. They meant Ms. Turner was going to give a pop quiz.

"Since the science fair is tomorrow, we're going to review the key terms for your projects," the teacher continued. "If the judges ask you to explain a term, you'll need to be ready.

When I say each word, please write down the definition."

Jake's face scrunched into a worried frown. He'd been totally stumped when he saw the science-fair words on the instructions. All those times he'd waved the instructions at Sir Isaac instead of reading them—

Jake closed his eyes. He could picture the instructions in Sir Isaac and Miss Earhart's workshop under his bed. If only he could remember what they said!

"'Hypothesis,'" Ms. Turner announced.

Jake tried to think. Was it H-I-P or H-Y-P? He glanced at the red numbers on the clock, a blur as the milliseconds slipped away . . .

"'Hypothesis,'" repeated Ms. Turner.

Hipothesis, Jake scribbled. Then he frowned. It didn't look right. Without even bothering to erase, he quickly changed the first "I" to a "Y." But spelling "hypothesis" wasn't even the hardest part. Now he had to *define* it.

Jake gnawed on the end of his pencil. *A hypothesis is a kind of guess*, he wrote. *A guess that scientists make about something they think will happen.*

Jake stared at his answer, trying to think of something else to write. He heard everybody else's pencils scratching, scratching . . .

And then he heard something else.

Z-z-z-z-z-z—zip.

Jake froze.

That sound—it was coming from under his desk.

It was coming from his backpack!

No, Jake thought desperately. *No, no, no, no!*

There was only one possible explanation for why his backpack would unzip itself.

Sir Isaac and Miss Earhart were trying to escape!

What am I going to do? Jake wondered, trying not to panic.

But the whole class was in the middle of taking a quiz. He couldn't exactly start talking to his backpack without attracting attention.

"The next word is 'procedure,'" Ms. Turner announced.

Jake's fidgety hand jerked forward. It bumped his pencil and sent it clattering to the floor—right under his desk. Luckily, Ms. Turner noticed. She nodded at Jake so that he knew he had permission to get it.

Jake dove under his desk. His backpack was already unzipped two inches! He stuck his face near the opening and hissed, "What are you *doing*?"

"We need air," Sir Isaac said with a scowl. "It is oppressively hot in here. And this satchel of yours carries the distinct odor of—"

"Feet." Miss Earhart spoke up.

"Just deal with it," Jake said through gritted teeth. "Stay put—and no more unzipping."

With a fast tug on the zipper, Jake returned to his seat. He started scribbling *pro*—

Zzzzzzzzzzip!

Not again, Jake thought. With his foot, he tried to move his backpack under the chair.

Across the aisle, Aiden glanced at Jake and frowned. Jake stared hard at his paper. He wasn't even finished writing "procedure" when Ms. Turner announced the next word. "'Investigation.'"

Jake knew that he had no choice but to move on. He shifted his feet to push the backpack again. The buckles on the straps clacked against the tile floor.

"Ms. Turner!" Aiden's hand shot into the air.

Everyone turned to look at him. Jake slouched low in his seat, wishing he could use mind control to keep Sir Isaac and Miss Earhart in his backpack.

"Yes, Aiden?" Ms. Turner asked. "Is there a problem?"

"Jake's fidgeting and it's really distracting," Aiden replied.

"I am not!" Jake protested.

A pinched look crossed Ms. Turner's face. "Aiden, keep your eyes on your own paper and you won't notice any distractions," she replied. "Now, back to the quiz. The next word is 'process.'"

Luckily, there were only two more words after "process." At last, Ms. Turner announced, "Please pass your papers forward."

Jake passed his quiz to the person who sat in front of him. Another F, he was sure . . . and Jake had a terrible feeling that his day was only going to get worse.

CHAPTER 9

"Next, we'll watch a video from last year's science fair so that you'll know what to expect," Ms. Turner told the class.

Jake breathed a sigh of relief as Ms. Turner turned out the lights and started a video on the SMART Board. Then Jake felt something tug on a leg of his jeans.

With a sinking feeling, Jake looked down. Sir

Isaac had poked his head out of the backpack—and was trying to get Jake's attention!

Jake shook his head. But Sir Isaac wouldn't take no for an answer. Even worse, Miss Earhart was peeking out of the bag, too!

With one swift motion, Jake leaned over, scooped both geniuses into his hand, and hid them in his desk.

"Please," he whispered. "You have to stop!"

But Sir Isaac wasn't listening, as usual. His eyes were wide with wonder as he peered around Jake, eager to see everything in the classroom. "This is your *schoolroom*?" He asked.

"Isaac," Miss Earhart said in a hushed voice, "I think you'd better—"

"What is *that*?" Sir Isaac exclaimed.

Jake glanced over his shoulder to see what Sir Isaac was pointing at. "The model of the solar system?" he guessed. He wasn't surprised that it had caught Sir Isaac's eye. The vibrant planets traveled on motorized tracks around a glittering golden sun.

"The sun *is* at the center!" Sir Isaac gasped. "Galileo and Copernicus were right! And—and—and are the planets traveling in *ellipses*?"

"In ovals?" Jake said. "Yeah, those are their orbits."

"Kepler would be pleased to know his theory of planetary motion was correct," Sir Isaac said approvingly. "But there are too many heavenly bodies displayed. There are but six in our solar system."

"Actually—" Jake began.

Sir Isaac didn't let him finish. "Unless—" he sputtered excitedly, "unless this means that there are even *more* planets than we knew—"

"Yes," Miss Earhart told him. "That's exactly what it means. Now, Isaac, we both promised Jake—"

"I must see for myself," Sir Isaac declared. His eyes were wild with delight.

"Absolutely not," Jake replied at once. "After school you can find out everything you want to know about the solar system, I promise. You just have to wait—"

Sir Isaac was inching toward the edge of the desk. "You ask me to wait?" he said incredulously. "I *have* waited, boy. I've spent my life waiting, watching, wondering. Searching for answers to questions no one else dared to ask. And now, with the truth hovering right overhead, you want me to stay quiet?"

"That's not—"

"I must investigate!" Sir Isaac insisted. The hint of a smile flickered across his face. "You are, perhaps, too young to understand," he said. "Perhaps being born in a time when so much is already known has diminished your curiosity. But I must have a closer look." Then he slid down the leg of the desk and darted across the floor.

Jake gasped and glanced around frantically.

Everyone else's eyes were on the SMART Board—but for how long? From the corner of his eye, Jake could see Sir Isaac shinny up the bookshelf and start climbing the blinds like a ladder.

Oh no, Jake thought in despair.

"Don't worry, Jake," Miss Earhart whispered, as if she could read his mind. "I'll bring him back!"

"No!" Jake squeaked as loud as he dared. But it was too late. Miss Earhart had already leaped to the floor! She zigged and zagged, dodging chairs and backpacks on her way to the same bookcase Sir Isaac had scaled.

Jake could only watch in horror as Miss Earhart began to climb the blinds, too. The thin aluminum strips rattled faintly, but to Jake they sounded like a sonic boom. How was it possible that nobody else had noticed?

Soon Sir Isaac reached the top of the blinds. In the dim room, Jake could just make out his silhouette as he reached, reached, *reeeeeeached* for the model . . .

Without warning, Sir Isaac leaped from the blinds! As he sailed through the air, Jake sucked in his breath so sharply that Aiden gave him a weird look. Just before he started to fall, Sir Isaac grabbed the wire with one tiny hand!

Jake could barely stand to look. But he forced himself to take another peek, just in time to see Miss Earhart give him an enthusiastic thumbs-up. He shook his head back and forth to stop her, but maybe Miss Earhart couldn't see him. Because the next thing Jake knew, she had cata-pulted through the air like Sir Isaac.

Now both geniuses were dangling from the solar system!

The force of their wild leaps made the model start wobbling. Hand over hand, Sir Isaac moved closer to the glittering sun, with Miss Earhart right behind him. The planets, dangling from delicate threads, began to sway as the wobbling got worse.

Jake didn't know what to do. Any minute now the video would end . . . the lights would go on . . . and the entire class would see the solar system model spinning out of control—with two tiny geniuses hanging on for dear life!

Jake had to do something. But what?

Just then, the video ended. "Emerson, would you please turn on the lights?" Ms. Turner asked.

It was now or never.

Jake took a deep breath, mustered all his courage, and took a running leap at the solar system model. There was enough light for him to see Sir Isaac and Miss Earhart, who were still dangling from the wire. Jake grabbed them and stuffed them in his pockets, where the heavy denim of his jeans muffled Sir Isaac's shouts of outrage.

The room was flooded with light just in time for everyone to see Jake land on the floor with a hard *thump*.

Then the solar system crashed on top of him!

"Jake Everdale!" Ms. Turner exclaimed. "What on earth is going on?"

Jake stared at the floor. The model of planet Earth had a big dent in Antarctica now, but he knew that wasn't what Ms. Turner meant.

"Stand up," Ms. Turner ordered him. "What are you doing?"

Jake pulled himself to his feet. "I . . ." he began. "Uh . . . I saw a . . . bee?"

"A bee?" Ms. Turner repeated.

"Yeah," Jake said, thinking fast. "I didn't want anyone . . . to get . . . stung. Ow!"

Jake didn't know for sure, but he was pretty sure that Sir Isaac had just kicked him!

The class erupted into giggles.

"I don't see any bees," Aiden said.

Ms. Turner sighed. "Hannah, please switch seats with Jake," she said. "Jake, you might find there are fewer distractions in the front row."

"But what about the solar system model?" Aiden asked. "Jake wrecked it!"

"I'm sorry," Jake said quickly. "I'll take it home and fix it. I promise."

Ms. Turner was quiet for a long moment. "Okay," she finally said. "I think that's a good idea. Now, if we could get back to discussing tomorrow's science fair . . . Does anyone have any questions?"

Jake kept his mouth pressed shut as he carried his notebook and backpack to the front of the room. Sitting at Hannah's old desk, in the center of the front row, he felt like he was in the middle of a fishbowl with everyone watching him. If Sir Isaac or Miss Earhart tried to escape again . . .

Jake couldn't bear to think about it.

CHAPTER 10

Miss Earhart must've given Sir Isaac a *serious* lecture, because the rest of the day passed without any more trouble. Jake knew better than to push his luck. At 3:00:00:00, he bolted from Franklin Elementary School with his backpack slung over one arm and the broken model of the solar system tucked under the other. As soon as Jake made it to the safety of his bedroom, he unzipped his backpack. "What were you thinking?" he exploded.

Miss Earhart and Sir Isaac clambered out.

"Why didn't you listen? I was trying to keep you safe!" Jake continued.

"But, Jake, there's so much more that deserves consideration," Miss Earhart spoke up. "The chance to explore—"

"To investigate," added Sir Isaac.

"To discover," they said at the same time. And then, to Jake's astonishment, they exchanged a smile.

Jake, however, didn't have anything to smile about. His shoulders slumped as he sat on the bed. "For you, maybe," he said. "But I have a huge science project due *tomorrow*, with a report and a presentation and everything. It's not even close to being ready. And I failed another quiz today while you two were trying to *explore* or *investigate* or whatever. Now I'm going to fail the science fair, too, which means I'll have to quit the baseball team."

There was a long pause, then Miss Earhart and Sir Isaac started whispering frantically.

"Actually, Jake," Miss Earhart began, "that's not *quite* accurate."

"What do you mean?" he replied.

Miss Earhart smiled mysteriously. "Close your eyes," she said.

Why not? Jake thought as he shut his eyes. Then he heard an unfamiliar sound coming from under his bed—a sputtering kind of sound—followed by—

Was that a *burning* smell?

Jake sniffed frantically as Flapjack started whining at the door. "Oh no," Jake muttered. "Not again!"

He dropped to the floor and lifted the blanket.

Whoosh!

Something flew out from under the bed, so close to Jake's head that it buzzed the edges of his hair. He leaped up—never, never, never had he expected to see anything like this—

Amelia Earhart, the world-famous pilot, was flying around his room!

She threw back her head and laughed with glee as she expertly piloted the plane, swooping under and over the paper-clip garlands without hitting a single one. Sir Isaac watched in astonishment as Miss Earhart did a loop in midair. Still grinning, Miss Earhart began to descend, gliding in for a flawless landing on Jake's desk.

"Surprise!" Miss Earhart exclaimed as she climbed out of the plane. "Not too shabby, eh? What do you think?"

"It's amazing!" Jake gasped, crouching down to get a closer look. The plane was about eight inches long, with a propeller made of Popsicle sticks. The delicate frame was constructed from stretched-out paper clips, with broad wings that had been covered in canvas—Jake hardly minded when he realized that the canvas scraps had been cut from his baseball-gear bag. With the tip of his pinkie finger, Jake flicked open the engine compartment. A gleaming engine—built from a pair of bottle caps, Flapjack's old tags, stripped twist ties, and a miniature spring—was still radiating heat. In the open-air cockpit, Jake could even see a pair of tiny safety harnesses made from rubber bands!

"When did you *do* this?" Jake asked.

"I'll be honest, we burned the midnight oil," Miss Earhart replied, covering a yawn with her hand. Then she noticed the alarm on Jake's face. "It's an expression! It means we stayed up too late. I promise we didn't burn anything else."

"How can I thank you?" Jake asked Miss Earhart and Sir Isaac. "This is incredible! All I have to do now is write the report—"

"Ahem." Sir Isaac spoke up. With a flourish, he presented Jake with a stack of tiny pages.

"You wrote the report, too?" Jake exclaimed. "It's all done?"

"Everything except the trifold poster," Miss Earhart said. "That was a little too big for us to handle."

"I don't know what to say," Jake said. "Thank you! Thank you *so* much!" He used his thumb and forefinger to pinch the papers. "I'll just copy this onto something bigger and it will be good to go."

"If you have difficulty deciphering any of the equations, I shall be happy to advise," Sir Isaac said.

Jake got out a stack of lined paper and his favorite pencil. He squinted at the tiny pages, then began to write:

Flight! Whosoever could imagine that such a feat could be accomplished by man? And yet it is so! The chains of Gravity have been smashed, if only momentarily. The principles behind such are not overly complex, and yet

Jake paused.

And yet.

He put down his pencil.

And yet . . . It wasn't just that Jake didn't understand everything Sir Isaac had written in the report. It wasn't just that his words sounded nothing like the way Jake would write. It was the fact that this project wasn't Jake's work.

It didn't matter, Jake suddenly realized, if he copied it over in his own handwriting. It didn't even matter if he fooled everyone at Franklin Elementary School. In his heart, Jake knew—and would always know—that he had cheated. It was an icky, squirmy kind of feeling that was even worse than the dread Jake felt during a quiz. And in that moment, Jake realized something important.

I might be a failure, Jake thought, *but I'll never be a cheater.*

Jake wasn't happy, exactly. How could he be, when tomorrow he'd have to tell Coach Carlson that he was leaving the team? But in a strange way, he was relieved.

He leaned over to the little plane and twirled the tiny propeller. It was an amazing invention, and Jake's only regret was that he couldn't show it off to everyone at school tomorrow. He'd have to ask Miss Earhart and Sir Isaac to explain how they built it. Jake grinned as he remembered watching Miss Earhart fly the plane around his room. *I wonder how she nailed all those turns*, he thought. Last year, Jake had thrown a paper airplane at Emerson in the lunchroom. To his surprise, the airplane flew higher and farther than he expected, landing in the Tater Tots! Everybody laughed, but the cafeteria monitor was *so mad* she threatened to take Tots off the menu for a whole month. *Why did my plane fly like that?* Jake wondered.

Suddenly, he remembered what Sir Isaac had said about not being curious. Jake was plenty curious about all sorts of stuff. And if curiosity was what he *really* needed to get started on his science project . . .

Jake reached for his pencil.

What ~~things~~

What forces affect how a paper airplane flies?

Is it the folds?

Is it the kind of paper?

Is it the weather?

Is it how you throw the plane?

Jake read over the questions. He had a feeling that he was on his way to developing the purpose of his science project. Next would be the hypothesis—but first, he needed to do a little research.

"Miss Earhart?" Jake called. "How do airplanes fly anyway?"

A broad smile spread across Miss Earhart's face. "Why, Jake," she replied, "I thought you'd never ask."

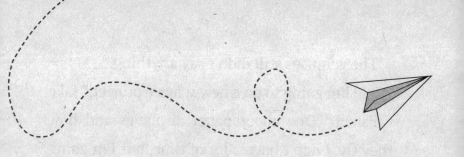

CHAPTER 11

"Let's start with the propeller," Miss Earhart said.

Jake held up his hand. "Actually, I should've said *paper* airplanes," he told her. "I need to change my science project."

Miss Earhart and Sir Isaac exchanged a glance.

"I'm starting over," Jake explained. "The plane you built is *amazing*. I don't even know how to thank you for all your work. But that's the problem—it's your work. Not mine."

The geniuses still didn't say anything.

"So I'm going to do a new science project," Jake finished. "One about paper airplanes and how they fly. I don't have a lot of time, but I'm going to try my best."

"Which is all we ever can do, really," Miss Earhart said.

"I respect your decision, boy," Sir Isaac said. "What sort of experiments do you plan to conduct?"

"I'm going to make different kinds of paper airplanes," Jake said. "Then I'll test them to see how well each one flies. And—I'll research the stuff that affects how a plane flies."

"Write this down," Miss Earhart said. "You'll want to learn about force."

Sir Isaac's face brightened. "Allow me, madam," he said. "Perhaps you've heard of my laws of motion?"

"Uh . . ." Jake said, a blank look on his face.

For once, Sir Isaac didn't look annoyed. "My first law of motion," he declared. "Objects in motion stay in motion, while objects at rest stay at rest, unless acted upon by a force."

"He means that things that are moving will stay moving unless something stops them," Miss Earhart translated. "And things that *aren't* moving won't move unless something makes them."

"That's what I said!" Sir Isaac objected. "Now, my second law of motion stems from the first. It is this: An object's acceleration is reliant on its mass and the force exerted upon it."

"And *that* means, simply enough, that an object will move if force is applied to it," Miss Earhart piped up. "How much force you need to use depends on how heavy the object is and how fast it's going."

Jake, who had been writing every word, paused. "That makes sense," he said. "Obviously, it takes more force to move a brick than a feather."

"And, of course, the third law of motion: For every action, there is an equal and opposite reaction," Sir Isaac said.

"Here's an example," Miss Earhart said. "If my action is to bounce a ball on the ground, the ground's reaction will push the ball back up. Does that make sense?"

"Kind of," Jake said, staring at his notebook.

"I'm sure it will become clear as you do your research. Here are some aerodynamics terms to look up, too," Miss Earhart said. " 'Drag.' 'Weight.' 'Thrust.' And, of course, 'lift.' "

Jake wrote each one down.

"Now, how can we help?" Miss Earhart continued. "Perhaps we could gather supplies or—"

"No!" Jake exclaimed. The last thing he needed was Sir Isaac and Miss Earhart roaming around the house again. "I mean, no thank you. You've already done so much."

"We could try our hand at repairing the solar system," Sir Isaac suggested with a longing glance at the model. Jake tried to hide his smile. He had a funny feeling that Sir Isaac would do just about anything for the chance to study it up close.

"Excellent suggestion!" Miss Earhart agreed. "After all, it's our fault that it broke."

Jake spent the rest of the evening doing searches on the computer and writing down lots of notes about everything he learned. At bedtime, he changed into his pajamas, brushed his teeth, and said good night to his parents—but he didn't get into bed. That was when the fun part started!

Jake went right to work making paper airplanes. There was one made of stiff construction paper and one made of shiny wrapping paper that was covered with pictures of superheroes and light-ning bolts. He took an empty cereal box out of the recycle bin to make a cardboard airplane. He even made a plane out of a flimsy square of toilet paper! Then Jake snuck downstairs and nabbed a package of printer paper from Dad's office. He used it to make a few dozen airplanes, each with its own unique twist.

Every so often, Jake snuck a glance at Sir Isaac and Miss Earhart, who were talking quietly as they put the model of the solar system back together. He could only imagine what they were discussing. As much as he wanted to know, though, Jake knew he had to focus on his project.

The moon gleamed high in the night sky when Jake finally climbed into bed. His trifold poster lay flat on his desk so that the glue could dry. He'd written every section of his report except the cover page. *I'll do it in the morning*, Jake thought sleepily. He crawled into bed and turned off the light . . .

Click!

"Sir Isaac. *Please*," Jake groaned as he pulled the pillow over his head. "I *have* to sleep, the science fair is *tomorrow—*"

"Actually, it's today," Sir Isaac interrupted him.

"Rise and shine!" Miss Earhart added, sounding entirely too cheerful.

Jake squinted as he tried to read the clock. It read 7:35. That was all it took for his eyes to pop wide open. He flung back the blankets. Ready or not, the science fair was *today*!

Jake pulled on his favorite green T-shirt and his lucky baseball socks. Ordinarily, Jake would only wear them on game day—but he wasn't taking any chances. He scribbled a cover page for the report and packed his paper airplanes in a shoe box. He was about to head downstairs when, at the last minute, he decided to take the stack of extra printer paper with him.

Before he left the room, Jake paused in the doorway. It seemed rude to leave for the science fair without inviting Miss Earhart and Sir Isaac, after all they'd done for him. "Do you want—" he began.

Behind Sir Isaac, Miss Earhart started waving her arms wildly to get Jake's attention. She shook her head "no" so hard that her short curls flew back and forth as she pointed at Sir Isaac. Suddenly, Jake could just picture how Sir Isaac would react to a science fair with dozens and dozens of experiments—some of them containing technology he'd never seen, or information he'd never dreamed could be true. Jake could almost see Sir Isaac bounding from display to display . . .

And hear the shrieks from Franklin Elementary School's students and teachers . . .

"—me to leave the light on?" Jake finished.

"Yes, yes, that will be fine," Sir Isaac said. "I do have a few more experiments I'd like to conduct."

"Good luck, Jake!" Miss Earhart said as she waved.

Just then, Mom appeared at the foot of the stairs. "Ready to go?" she asked, jingling her car keys. "I thought you could use a ride to school today."

"Thanks," Jake replied gratefully.

Instead of dropping Jake off in front of the school, Mom drove him to the side entrance so Jake would be closer to the gym. Out of the corner of his eye, Jake could see the janitor unlocking the gate at Franklin Fields. Just beyond, he knew, was the storm drain that had started it all.

"Good luck today," Mom said. "Dad and Julia and I will be there!"

Jake smiled in response, even though the thought of an audience only made him more nervous. He was halfway to the gym when he heard Mom yell, "Jake! Wait!"

"I'm so proud of you," she called through the open car window. "I know you'll do great!"

"Thanks, Mom," Jake replied.

Then he continued on to the gym.

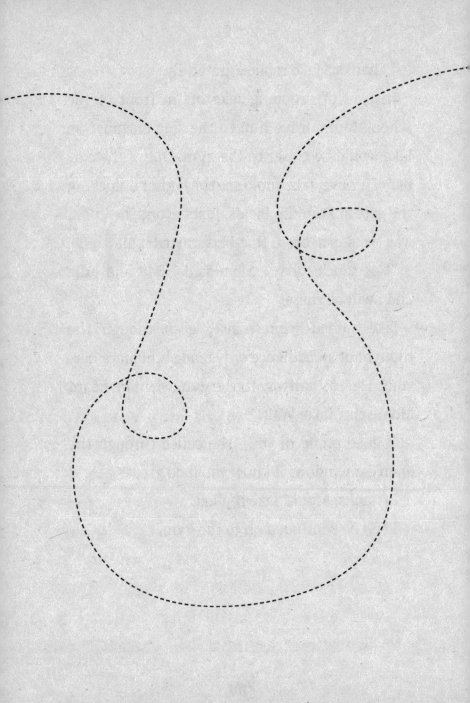

CHAPTER 12

When Jake stepped into the gym, his mouth dropped open. It had been transformed! An enormous banner read FRANKLIN ELEMENTARY SCHOOL SCIENCE FAIR. The gym buzzed with activity as students set up their science fair projects.

"Jake!"

It was Emerson. He ran up to Jake with a huge grin on his face. "Isn't this awesome? Clara did a project about stuff that glows in the dark, and Aiden, it's so crazy, he made an actual working model of the human digestive system!"

"Wow," Jake said. "Those projects sound cool."

But what he thought was, *A lot cooler than my paper airplane project.*

Jake glanced behind him just in time to see Mom's car disappear—along with every wild, last-ditch hope he had of disappearing with it.

"Come on," Emerson said. "Our class has a bunch of tables together. I saved one for you, right next to me."

Jake followed Emerson to an empty table and unfolded his poster. Then the warning bell rang. Jake knew he had to move fast. He tucked the extra paper and the shoe box of airplanes behind his poster so no one would mess with them. Without his planes on display, Jake's table looked especially bare.

After Jake got to class, it was even harder to

concentrate than usual. At least, sitting in the front row, he didn't have to see Aiden's smug face smirking at him. The red numbers on the clock kept moving, just like always. At 2:59:30:01, Principal Barron's voice crackled over the loudspeaker. "Greetings, teachers and students," he announced. "It's my pleasure to invite all of you to the Franklin Elementary School Science Fair, starting . . . *now!*"

At that moment, the bell echoed through the classroom. The school day was over . . . and the science fair was about to begin!

The hallway that led to the gym was crowded with parents who had to wait outside until after the students presented their projects to the judges. In the gym, Jake watched nervously as Principal Barron and the judges walked down the aisle, stopping at each project. Elizabeth's volcano . . . Marco's ant farm . . . Hannah's seedlings . . . Aiden's model of the digestive system . . .

Jake watched out of the corner of his eye as Aiden poured a cup of gloppy liquid into the model's mouth. Suddenly, there was a gasp of surprise— the judges all jumped back—

Emerson doubled over with laughter. "Did you see that?" he howled. "Aiden's project just puked on the judges' shoes!"

Jake tried to smile, but he felt like *he* might puke if he opened his mouth.

Emerson quickly stopped laughing as the judges approached his table. "My name is Emerson Lewis, and my project is about the weather," he began.

Jake could barely concentrate on Emerson's presentation, knowing that in just moments, the judges would approach him. They seemed to like Emerson's project. Jake saw them smiling and nodding their heads. Principal Barron wrote a few notes in his notebook.

Then the judges started moving again—right toward Jake.

Jake took a deep breath.

"My name is Jake Everdale, and my project is called Fly or Fall," he said. "Flight is something we take for granted. But for thousands of years, people used to dream of the day when it would be possible for humans to fly. Sir Isaac Newton came up with the theory of gravity and figured out the three laws of motion. Pioneers like Amelia Earhart took the big risks that helped us learn more about how planes could fly. But how, exactly, do planes stay in the air?"

Jake paused to take another deep breath. The judges were listening to him with friendly smiles.

"There are four things that really affect how a plane flies," Jake continued. "Weight pulls the plane downward with a little help from our friend, gravity—a force that was first described by the one and only Sir Isaac Newton. Lift, on the other hand, does the opposite. As air currents move over and under the plane's wings, they pull the plane *up, up, up and away!*"

Jake made some funny sound effects as he demonstrated. Emerson cracked up, just like Jake knew he would. But the judges chuckled, too—and not in a bad way. That made Jake feel even more encouraged.

"Drag is the force that pulls the plane backward—or slows it down—as it flies through the air," Jake told the crowd. "And thrust is what moves the plane forward. In a real one, that's the engine's job. But for a paper airplane"—Jake paused to clench his arm into a muscle, making everyone laugh again—"that's my job.

"These forces don't just affect jumbo jets and space shuttles," Jake explained. "They affect paper airplanes, too. Which means that different folds and designs can change how paper airplanes fly. Adding fins to the wings or the tail helps a paper airplane not crash. A little weight to the nose of the plane makes it more stable. If the wings are weak, you can make them stronger by adding an extra fold or two. Like this."

The judges leaned forward to watch Jake's paper airplane demonstration—and so did the kids. He had everyone's complete attention.

The first plane Jake made was simple—just five basic folds. The other plane started the same way, but then Jake made a few adjustments. A couple of extra folds gave the wings fins, and with a square of paper and a piece of tape, Jake added one more fin to the tail of his plane. Finally, he added a shiny silver paper clip to the plane's nose. At last, his planes were ready.

But would they work?

As Jake stepped into the aisle, the crowd parted. He took a deep breath—

Aimed the planes—

And launched them!

The first plane veered to the left and crashed into Emerson's poster. But the second plane soared effortlessly through the air before gliding to a landing several feet away. Jake pumped his fist in the air. He'd done it! He'd proved his hypothesis!

The whole crowd started to clap.

"Well done, Jake," Principal Barron said. "Do you mind if I give it a try? I haven't flown a paper airplane in years."

"Of course," Jake replied. Then he gestured to the printer paper from Dad's office. "You could even make your own, if you want. I brought enough for everybody."

"Well . . . maybe just one," Principal Barron said as he eagerly reached for a piece of paper. That was all it took for a line to form—the other judges, the students, even the cafeteria lady took a turn, until every single page had been turned into a plane. Soon the air was filled with paper airplanes!

Jake grinned so hard his face hurt while he

watched. The entire school was flying paper planes, laughing and shrieking as the planes catapulted through the gym.

And the best part?

Jake's science project was the reason for it all!

CHAPTER 13

After the last paper airplane landed, the judges continued their tour of the science projects. Jake was only partly relieved. His presentation was over—thank goodness—but the judging, and his grade, were still to come.

At last, Principal Barron walked back to the microphone. The chatter in the gym immediately stopped. "Every year, this job gets harder and harder," he announced. "What an outstanding display of projects! Now, I must ask all the students to join your parents in the hall so that the judges can confer and award this year's prizes."

Mom, Dad, and Julia were waiting right outside the door. "Hey, champ!" Dad said as he clapped his hand on Jake's shoulder. "How did it go?"

Jake shrugged. "Pretty good, I guess. Principal Barron made his own paper airplane."

Mom and Dad looked surprised. "Did he?" Mom asked. "It sounds like your project was very inspiring."

"Aunt Margaret is so sorry she couldn't make it," Dad told Jake. "She said she knows you'll make the family proud."

I sure hope so, Jake thought.

After a few more minutes, the doors to the gym opened wide once more. The judges had finished evaluating the projects. Now it was time to find out who had won first, second, and third prize. Of course, Jake didn't really care about the ribbons.

He never expected to win one. That's why he didn't understand, at first, why there was a shiny red ribbon stuck on the corner of his poster. He blinked—stared at it—blinked again—

"Dude! You won second place! You won!" Emerson yelled excitedly. Then Mom and Dad were hugging Jake, and Julia was tugging on his hand, and Principal Barron was trying to shake his other hand. But Jake could only stare at the ribbon with a great big openmouthed grin.

I did it, Jake thought. *I passed!*

Now he could stay on the baseball team. Now he could tell Sir Isaac and Miss Earhart the best news ever. And now he knew that with a lot of hard work—and a little extra help—anything was possible!

"We're going out for dinner," Dad announced when Jake and his family got home later. "And then we'll go to Frosty's for dessert! But first, we have to tell Aunt Margaret. She'll be so excited to hear there's a budding scientist in the family!"

That reminded Jake about the geniuses upstairs. They would be excited to hear the news, too.

"Be right back," Jake murmured as he slipped away. He took the stairs two at a time and burst into his room—

"Look!" he said, holding out the shiny red ribbon. "I got second place!"

Miss Earhart and Sir Isaac were huddled together, deep in conversation. At the sound of Jake's voice, they both jumped up.

"I knew you could do it!" Miss Earhart said joyfully.

Sir Isaac's stern features softened for the first time. "Well done, boy," he said stiffly—but the gleam in his eyes gave away his pride.

"I couldn't have done it without you," Jake said. "You reminded me what the science fair was really about. I'm sorry that I couldn't show everyone the plane you built, though. I know they would've been so impressed."

Miss Earhart smiled brightly. "That's no matter," she replied. "We've had an idea for what to do with it."

"It seemed quite a shame to let the aircraft go to waste," Sir Isaac spoke up.

"What's your plan?" Jake asked.

Miss Earhart flung her arms wide, gesturing to the window. "We thought we'd set off on an adventure!"

Jake blinked. "You're . . . leaving?" he asked.

"That's right," Miss Earhart replied. She bent over the engine of the little plane, adjusting it with a pin. "We've just been doing the final calibrations. We should be ready to take off momentarily."

Jake could hardly believe that Sir Isaac and Miss Earhart would be gone soon. The geniuses had disrupted his life in just about every way imaginable. *It will be good for things to go back to normal*, Jake tried to tell himself. *Baseball and homework and all the regular stuff.*

The truth was, though, that Jake was going to miss them more than he could admit.

"How can I help?" he said suddenly.

Sir Isaac and Miss Earhart turned around to look at him.

"I know!" Jake exclaimed. "Batteries!"

He raced around his room, taking the batteries out of every toy he owned until there was a small mountain of them on the table.

"Take as many as you want," Jake told the geniuses. "They can be your backup power source."

"What will this modern world think of next?" Sir Isaac said, impressed. "Thank you, boy."

"No," Jake said. "Thank you. I learned so much from you—about being curious and asking questions and taking chances and looking for adventures. I won't forget it. Ever."

Miss Earhart reached out, took hold of Jake's finger, and shook. "And neither will we," she told him.

Then she turned to Sir Isaac. "Ready, Isaac?" she asked. "Would you like to give her a spin?"

Sir Isaac strode across the desk to the little plane. Just as he was about to climb into the pilot's seat, though, he hesitated. Then he turned back to Miss Earhart with a small bow. "Perhaps you should take the controls," he said. "I expect I still have a lot to learn."

Miss Earhart looked surprised, but only for a moment. Then she grinned, climbed into the cockpit, and snapped her goggles over her eyes. Sir Isaac settled into the seat next to her and fastened his safety harness.

The engine rumbled.

The Popsicle-stick propeller started spinning.

The airplane began to inch across Jake's desk, picking up speed—

"Wait!" Jake exclaimed. "Where will you go?"

Miss Earhart could barely hear him over the roar of the engine. "Go?" she repeated. "Wherever the wild winds take us, I suppose."

The plane lurched off the edge of the desk. It wobbled in midair for just a moment; then Miss Earhart pulled hard on the controls. The plane zoomed into the air, higher, faster, *faster*—

Jake ran across the room and opened the window just in time. The plane sailed outside into the clear blue sky.

"Good-bye, Jake!" Miss Earhart called, her white scarf fluttering in the wind. "Good-bye!"

Jake watched at the window until the tiny plane disappeared from sight. Just like that, the geniuses were gone, as suddenly and unexpectedly as they'd arrived. For a long moment, Jake stared at the empty sky. Had it really happened? It was almost too impossible to believe.

Then Jake turned around. He saw Julia's dollhouse with the toilet-paper curtains . . . the paper-clip chains of crystal beads . . . the melted crayons. The miniature workshop was still under his bed. And best of all, the satiny red SECOND PLACE ribbon was on his desk.

Yes. It had definitely happened.

But how?

"I wish—" Jake began, but quickly stopped himself. He wasn't quite ready to find out what would happen if he finished that sentence!

A NOTE FROM THE AUTHOR

Sir Isaac Newton was born on January 4, 1643, in Lincolnshire, England. He was born prematurely, so small that no one expected him to live more than a few hours. Amazingly, he did survive, and grew up to change our understanding of the world in ways that no one could have predicted. His astonishing survival was just a hint of the incredible things to come.

Sir Isaac didn't have an easy childhood. He was deeply lonely and got into fights with other boys at school. His mother hoped that her son would become a farmer, but he neglected his chores and got into even more trouble. All the while, young Isaac was keenly observing the world, preparing himself to answer questions that few people dared to even ask. His lifelong search for those answers led him to create the reflecting telescope, discover gravity, and develop the three laws of motion— scientific advancements that still benefit us today.

Not all of Sir Isaac's endeavors were successful, though. In his later years, he spent a tremendous amount of time on the study of alchemy, or how to turn ordinary substances into gold. After he died in 1727, his fellow scientists were embarrassed to find Sir Isaac's extensive notes on alchemy, and his writings were kept hidden for centuries. But scientific advancement depends on the desire to investigate new ideas, take risks, make mistakes, and believe in the impossible. We owe Sir Isaac Newton a great debt for his willingness to do just that.

Amelia Earhart was born on July 24, 1897, in Atchison, Kansas. Even as a child, her daring and love of adventure were on full display. Amelia was born in a time when very strict rules dictated what women should and should not do. She challenged those rules at every turn, making it possible not just for herself to live her dreams, but for other women as well.

During World War I, Amelia was so moved by

the suffering of wounded soldiers that she left college to work as a nurse's aide. After the war, she had her first airplane ride in 1920. Amelia was immediately captivated by the thrilling freedom of flight. She knew at once that becoming a pilot was what she wanted more than anything in the world. Amelia worked tirelessly to achieve her dream, even when others tried to stand in her way. She proved them all wrong by setting or breaking several records, including being the first woman to fly solo across the country.

Amelia's final flight, in 1937, was an attempt to fly around the entire world. Somewhere over the Pacific Ocean, though, something went terribly wrong, and Amelia and her copilot, Fred Noonan, vanished without a trace. To this day, no one knows what really happened, though new theories—and perhaps even new evidence—arise from time to time. The mystery behind Amelia's disappearance may never be solved, but her world-changing legacy lives on.